LOOK AND FIND®

ICE AGE 2™
THE MELTDOWN

Illustrated by Art Mawhinney
Cover inset illustrated by Blue Sky Studios

Published by
Louis Weber, C.E.O.
Publications International, Ltd.
7373 North Cicero Avenue
Lincolnwood, Illinois 60712

Ground Floor, 59 Gloucester Place
London W1U 8JJ

www.pilbooks.com

p i Kids is a registered trademark of
Publications International, Ltd.
Look and Find is a registered trademark of
Publications International, Ltd.

8 7 6 5 4 3 2 1

ISBN 1-4127-6062-3

Sid has started his own day camp for kids, but some might say that he acts more like a child than any of them. As Manny and Diego look on, see if you can find these young campers frolicking in the water park.

Rhino

Birdie

Diatryma

Beaver

Aardvark

Glypto

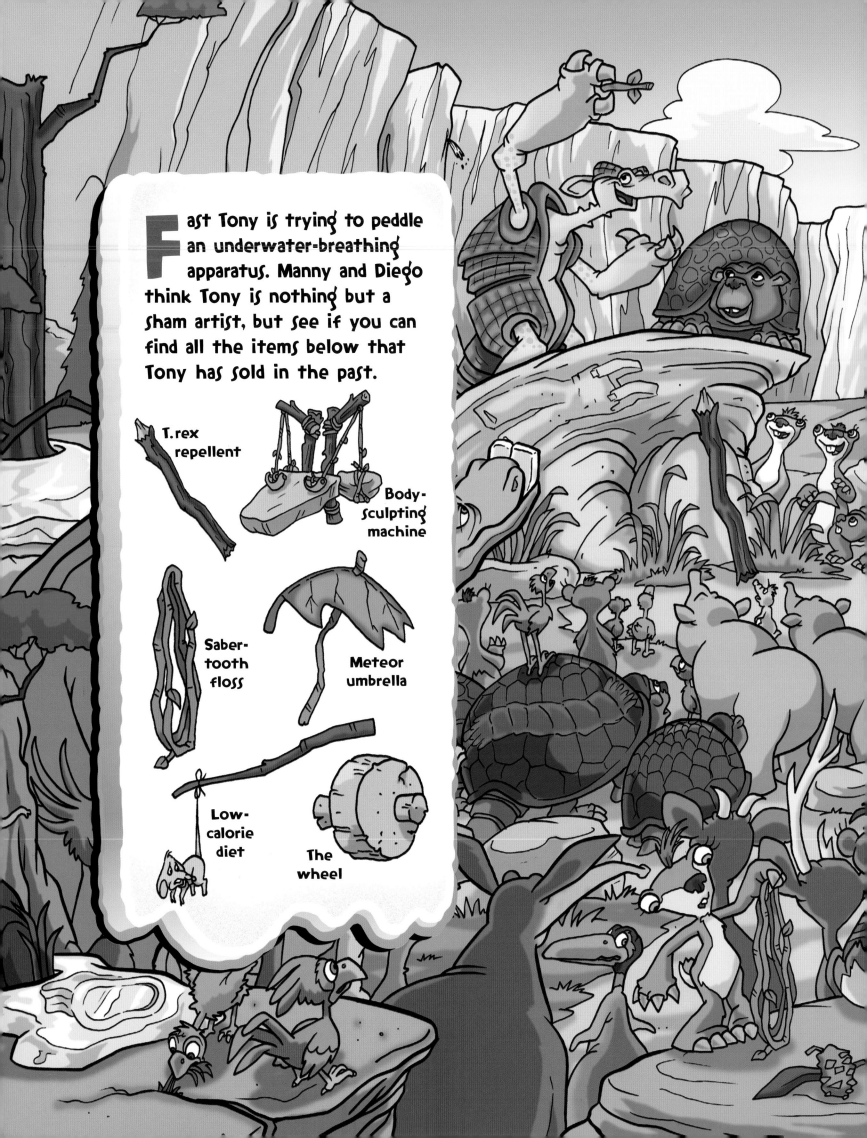

Fast Tony is trying to peddle an underwater-breathing apparatus. Manny and Diego think Tony is nothing but a sham artist, but see if you can find all the items below that Tony has sold in the past.

T.rex repellent

Body-sculpting machine

Saber-tooth floss

Meteor umbrella

Low-calorie diet

The wheel

If survival of the fittest has taught us anything, it's that you never mess with a saber-toothed squirrel's acorns. In order to defend the acorns he lost in the water, Scrat is prepared to karate chop these piranhas until his arms fall off. Swim around to find these other fish that didn't survive the Ice Age.

Clownaroundus sillymus

Tuxedous fancius

Stinkus reekus

Foureyeus blindus

Cluckus peckus

Abrahamus lincolnus

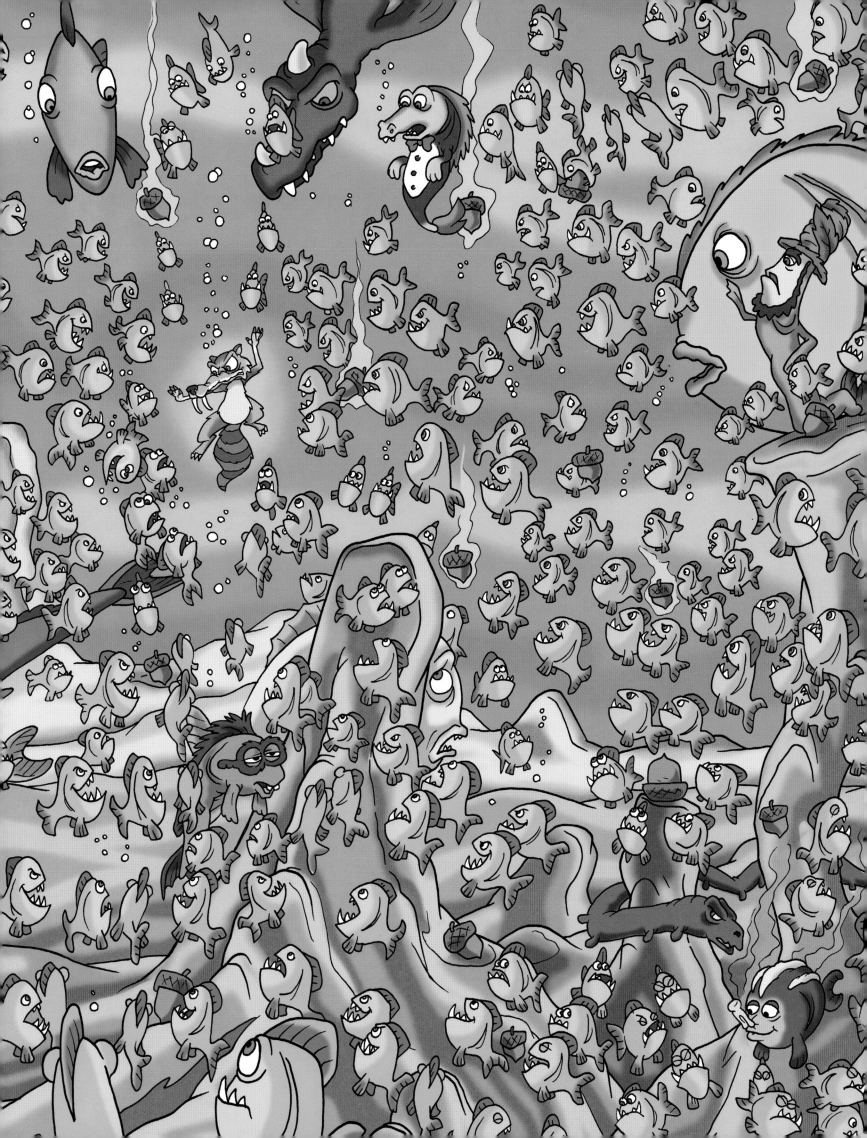

Just when everything seemed calm, our heroes were suddenly attacked by Maelstrom and Cretaceous. The villains broke the ice into hundreds of pieces, leaving Diego stranded on a small floating ice chunk—and Diego is afraid of water! Speaking of scared, see if you can find these other frightening shapes in the ice.

Spider

Clown

Gorilla

Ghost

Lightning

Shark

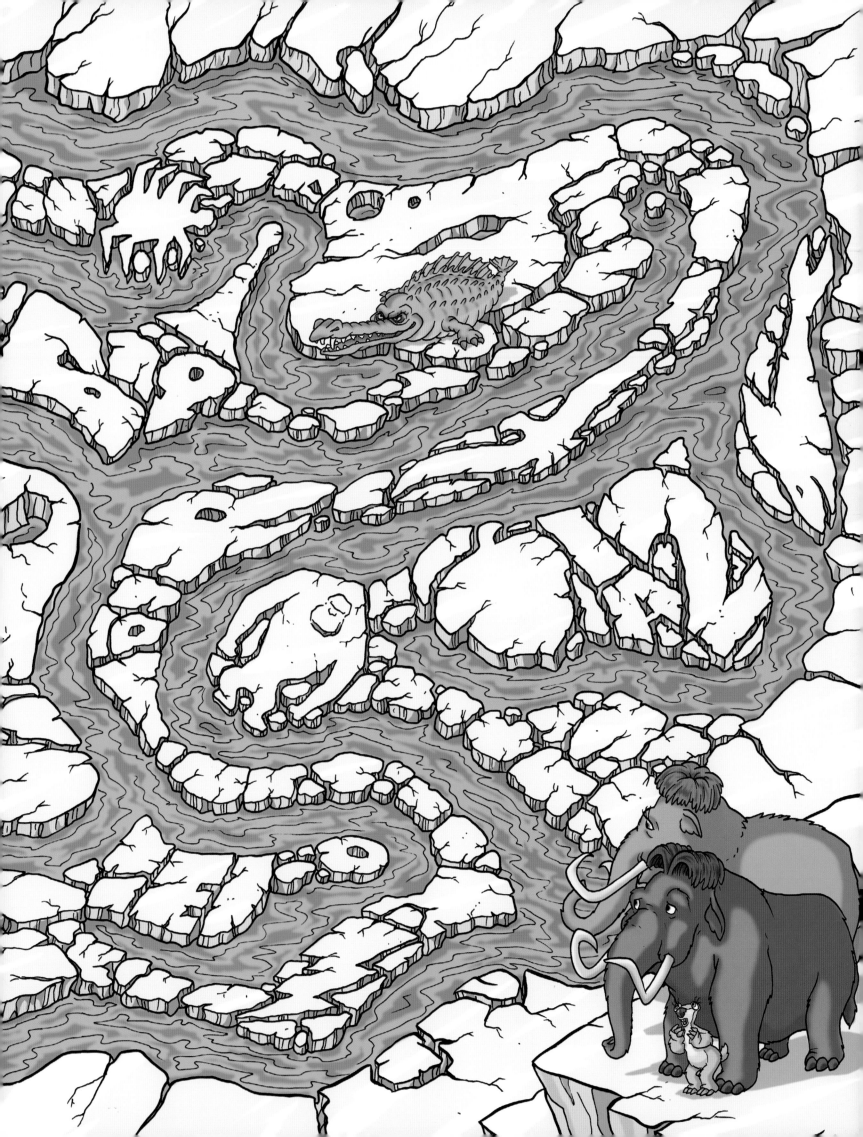

Never before had a place felt so much like home to Ellie and Manny. The Sacred Mammoth Grounds played host to many mammoth apparitions. See if you can find these shadowy figures floating in the evening sky.

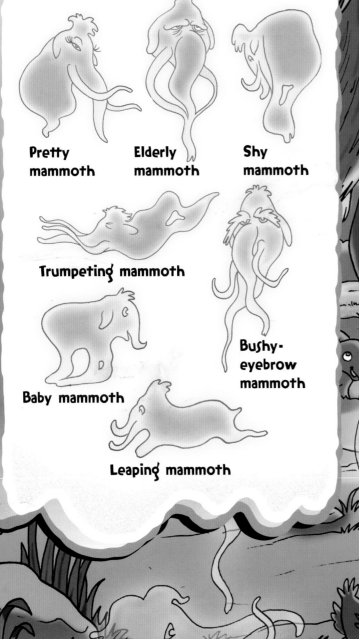

Pretty mammoth

Elderly mammoth

Shy mammoth

Trumpeting mammoth

Bushy-eyebrow mammoth

Baby mammoth

Leaping mammoth

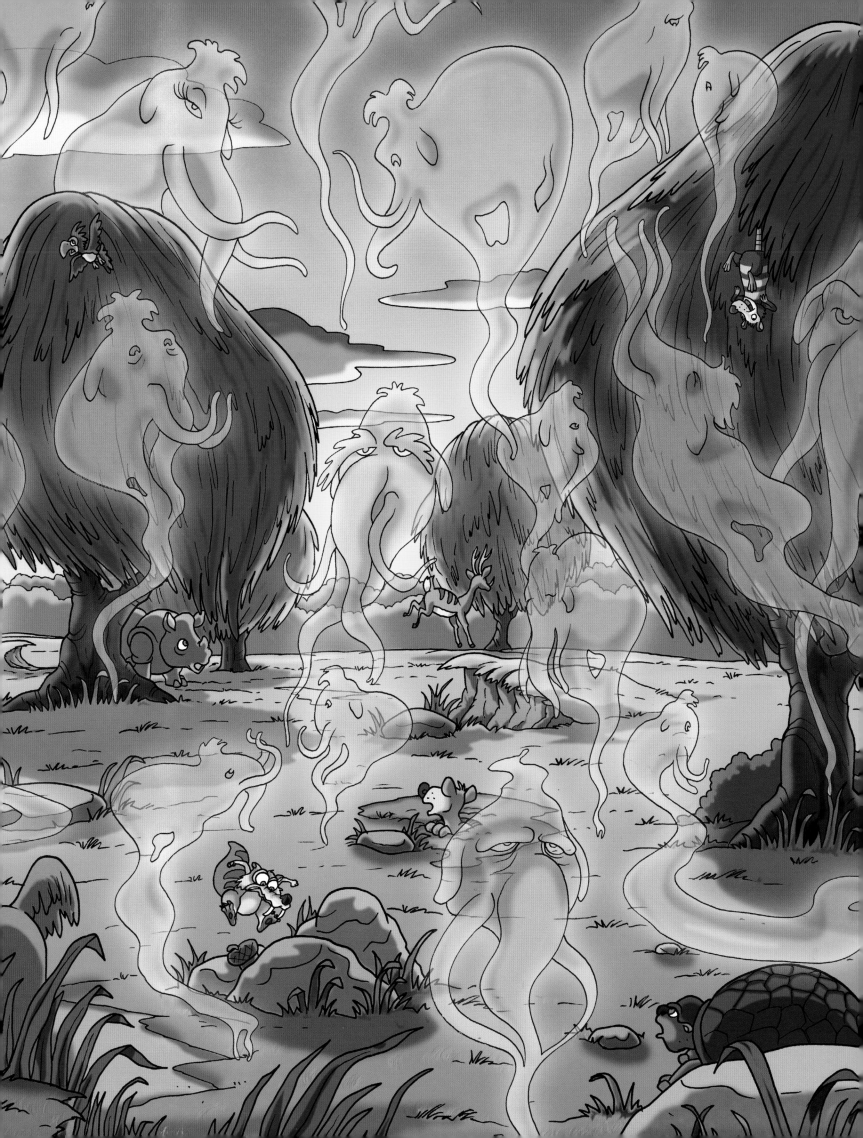

It's hard to believe why anyone would want to make Sid a god, but these colorful mini-sloths have done just that. Of course, they're going to throw him into a boiling tar pit, but still, they adore him. See if you can find all of these mini-sloths.

"Hooray for Sid!"

"Wow. Look at Sid!"

"Sid is dreamy."

"It's Sid. It's Sid. It's Sid."

"Sid is SO cool!"

"Whoa, that's Sid."

These geysers have created quite a roadblock for our heroes as they try to escape the flood that's coming. Every time a new one explodes it sends rocks flying everywhere! Manny, upset with Ellie, walks carelessly through them, but Sid and Diego fear for their lives. Find these boulders in the shapes of some familiar objects.

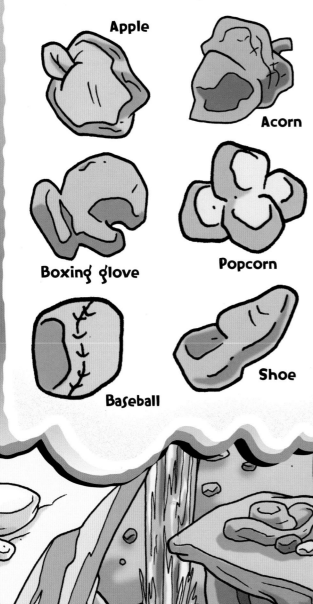

Apple

Acorn

Boxing glove

Popcorn

Baseball

Shoe

Our heroes thought that the journey to get to the sequoia boat was tough, but getting onboard was even harder. While Manny, Sid, and Diego try to make sure everyone gets onboard, see if you can find these other characters on or around the boat.

Fast Tony

Crash

Eddie

Cholly

Diatryma

Shovelmouth

What fun is a day at a water park without toys and other pool accessories? See if you can find these pool items as all the Ice Age families frolic and play.

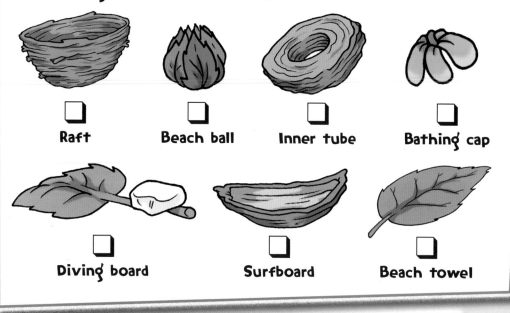

☐ Raft ☐ Beach ball ☐ Inner tube ☐ Bathing cap

☐ Diving board ☐ Surfboard ☐ Beach towel

Fast Tony is busy trying to hoodwink everyone into buying things they don't need. Look around the scene to find these impressions of objects that would have actually been useful in the Ice Age!

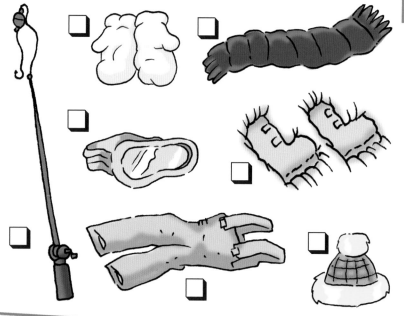

In the heat of his battle with all those ferocious piranhas, Scrat's acorns got away from him and drifted to all corners of the water's depths. See if you can find all 25.

Diego is stranded on a floating chunk of ice and he's afraid of the water. Help him get to safety by tracing a path through the ice to his friends. Be careful not to run into Cretaceous or Maelstrom.

Scrat has acorns on the brain and he's constantly trying to find and stash as many as he can. Scrat is somewhere in every scene. Go back and see if you can spot him trying to rescue all of his precious acorns.

The Mammoth Grounds are sacred for mammoths, and other creatures find the place peaceful as well. See if you can find these animals enjoying the sanctity of the grounds.

When the mini-sloths wanted to throw him into a tar pit, Sid was afraid that he was about to become extinct. Look in the smoky haze to find these creatures that really did go extinct.

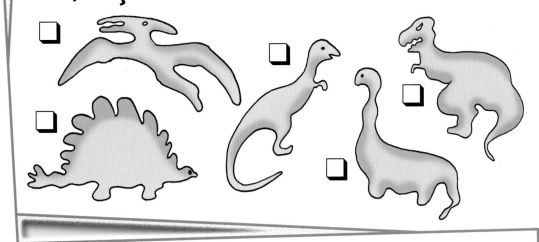

Our heroes had a hard time crossing the dangerous geyser fields— but they made it! Now go back and see if you can find these geysers with unique names. Here's a hint: they get their names from the way they look.

- [ ] The Hydrant
- [ ] The Fountain
- [ ] The Coyote
- [ ] The Popsicle
- [ ] The Whale
- [ ] Rusty

The gang finally made it to the boat safe and sound. But what's a trip on a cruise ship without entertainment? See if you can spot these silly animal entertainers.

| Stand-up chameleon | Performing tigers | Singing gorilla | Hula hippo | Juggling monkey | Show ostrich |